Gra... Kitchen

Happy Reading
Tricia Gardella

This is a work of fiction. Any similarity to any person living or dead is purely coincidental. The story is from the imagination of the author and all of the artwork was created by the illustrator. The story and artwork are the sole copyright of the author.

Published by Write 'em Cowgirl Publishing
To contact the author, write to the publisher at:
trigar@mlode.com

Copyright © Tricia Gardella

Grandma's Kitchen
by Tricia Gardella
Illustrated by Karen Donnelly

Category:
JUVENILE FICTION / Family

Paperback ISBN: 978-1-959412-09-0
Hardback ISBN: 978-1-959412-10-6
Library of Congress Control Number: 2023931413

Synopsis:
In this coming-of-age story, our young protagonist is told to bring along her sister this year. She is not happy. But soon she sees that canning tomatoes with Grandma is a step-by-step process, just like learning to share with your little sister.

WRITE 'EM COWGIRL PUBLISHING

Edited and designed by
Emerald Books
emerald-books.com

Grandma's Kitchen

by Tricia Gardella

Illustrated by Karen Donnelly

To Grandma Sarah, Oma —Tricia

To my own Little Helpers who are now pretty much grown. —Karen

One morning, Grandma calls.
She says, "I need my helper."

Then she says, "And bring Monica."

"She's too little," I complain.

"Bring Monica," Grandma says.

I run all the way down the hill to Grandma's. Monica almost keeps up.

Grandma is getting the buckets from the shed.
She gives us each a great big hug.
Then we go to the garden to pick.

Soon, tomatoes are piled up over the brim
of one bucket, and two more are half full.
That's when Grandma says, "That should do 'er."

When we get to the kitchen, Grandma wraps an apron around each of us.

Then we sort the tomatoes.

Grandma gives another wink and she says, "One pile of perfect like you, one pile for old ones like me."

She says the same thing every time.

In a little while, water is bubbling in a pot on the stove.

We wash the tomatoes, then Grandma plunges the firm ones, one at a time, in the boiling water—just for a minute.

She puts the dipped tomatoes in front of us.

"Watch," I tell Monica.

I pinch one. It squirts from its skin like a polliwog through my fingers.

Monica does one. She giggles. Monica's giggle makes me giggle. Grandma does too.

Into clean jars go the naked tomatoes, shoved in tighter than crayons in a box.

"A teaspoon of salt, then into the pot," Grandma says.

She puts the jars in front of me, and I screw on the lids.

Monica stands on her chair and watches.

"Here, you do one," I say.

Five jars take their boiling water bath in Grandma's canning pot.

The rest wait their turn on the counter.

Crank, crank, crank.

I grind the softer tomatoes through Grandma's special squeezer.

"My turn," says Monica.

Sssssspt! The squeezer spits tomato juice into Monica's eye.

Monica doesn't even cry. Grandma wipes her eye with a clean towel. I keep on grinding.

Monica looks at the pile on the counter through one eye. "It looks bigger than when we started," she complains.

"Watch," I say. "Mable, Mable, set the table, don't forget the red-hot pepper." Then I crank hot-pepper fast.

Sssssspt!

"Your turn," I tell Monica.

"One, two, buckle my shoe," Monica chants.

Then she cranks. Slowly. Slowly.

Grandma laughs.

Grandma. Monica. Me. Grandma. Monica. Me.

We each take a turn.

Soon juice and pulp are separated from seeds and skin.

The cranking seems to go faster this year.

Pip! Pop! Pip!

The jars on the table seal as they cool.

Now one canning pot and two tomato pots bubble on the stove. Grandma's kitchen feels warm and happy. Steamy tomato smells fill the air. Grandma skims liquid from both pots and sets it aside.

But it seems like forever before Grandma says, "Break time!"

She makes three sandwiches, then pours the saved juice into three cups. Monica takes a sip. I do too. The taste spreads on my tongue—sweet and tart at the same time.

"Not as good as lemonade," Monica says. That's what I thought the first time.

Now it tastes even better than lemonade to me.

Every few minutes, Grandma gets up to stir the pot and to change jars in the boiling water bath. Monica's head is down on the table. She is almost asleep.

But she jumps up when she hears Grandma say, "Sauce is ready."

"I wish I could do this forever," I say.

Grandma spoons the tomato sauce into small jars.

Monica and I put on the lids, and the jars take their place in line.

"Canning is hard work," Monica says.

"That's why there can never be too much help," Grandma says behind me.

I can feel her looking at me.

It seems like forever before all the jars have had their baths.

The sun is now on the other side of the house. Monica looks very tired. I pretend I'm not. I know there is more to do.

"Watch," I tell Monica.

I tap each jar lid with a spoon.

Pinka! Pinka! Pinka!

"That's good," I tell Monica. "Grandma says a **thop** means the jar didn't seal."

Monica plinks a tune on the lids, and I dance around the kitchen. Then Grandma dances over to the sink and pulls my chair with her.

"Time you took over another job," she says.

(moonwalk!)

Grandma carries the jars over to the sink.

I wash each jar. Monica dries them.

And Grandma puts labels on them.

Then I show Monica where they belong.

space for tomatoes!

The walls of Grandma's pantry are lined with shelves already packed with jam, green beans, corn relish, peppers, pickles, beets.

But there is still room for our tomatoes.

Monica's eyes slowly scan the shelves. "Did you help Grandma with all these?"

"Most of them," I say.

That's a lot of work," Monica says.

Grandma comes in and wraps her arms around Monica and me.

"A pretty good day's work," she says.

Monica looks at me.

"A pretty good year's work," she says.

Monica doesn't seem so little anymore.

"Maybe next year you can help with all of it," I say.

Then we give Grandma a great big hug,
and I take Monica's hand in mine as we head for home.

The End

About the Author

Tricia Gardella's books are mostly influenced by the ranch life she stepped into sixty years ago. She writes children's books about ranch animals, ranch routines, and ranch relationships, though she occasionally gets side-tracked to explore the myriad other sides of life. She has tried it all, and almost mastered some: canning, cooking, knitting and other fiber arts, rug-making, gardening, and various business ventures. But writing is her happiest of places and she is thrilled to be back after a twenty-year sabbatical. She has a BA in Ancient History and Classical Archaeology, three children, seven grandchildren, and three great grandchildren, all giving her much food for thought. She lives with two self-centered cats in Central California.

About the Illustrator

Karen Donnelly has been illustrating books and other things for many many years after a childhood spent drawing for fun, so she couldn't be happier. She lives near the sea with her family and dog who provide constant inspiration and interruptions.

WRITE 'EM COWGIRL PUBLISHING

triciagardella.com

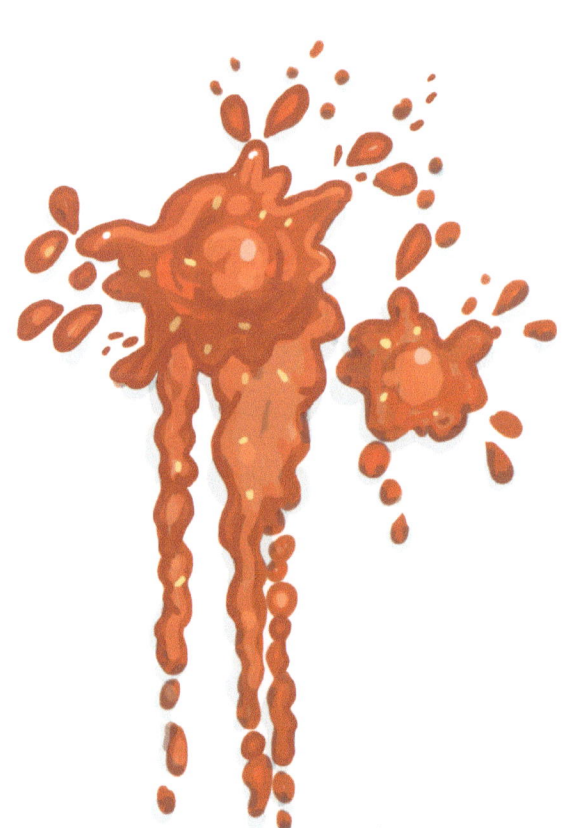

CPSIA information can be obtained
at www.ICGtesting.com
Printed in the USA
JSHW040949130323
38847JS00002B/6